MW01121096

The Legendary Unicorn

BY *Udo Weigelt*

ILLUSTRATED BY

Julia Gukova

Translated by J. Alison James

North-South Books

NEW YORK · LONDON

Every evening the animals met in a clearing in the forest to tell stories—fairy tales, myths, and legends—fantasies filled with magic and wonder.

One day, as Hedgehog was passing the stream on his way to the gathering, he saw an extraordinary creature leaning down to take a drink.

It was a unicorn! The hedgehog was astonished. All this time he had assumed that unicorns did not exist. Before the hedgehog could say a word, the unicorn disappeared.

Hedgehog ran off to tell the other animals.

"The unicorn is just a legend," argued Hare. "It is a fairy-tale animal. It's not real."

"But what I saw was real," insisted Hedgehog.

Bear didn't believe Hedgehog either. "The unicorn is a fabled creature, a myth," he said. "In reality there are no unicorns."

"What did I see then?" asked Hedgehog.

"Only leaves. Leaves and shadows of leaves," said Bear. "It was an illusion of a unicorn."

Not one single animal believed Hedgehog. Soon even he began to doubt that he'd actually seen a unicorn.

But on his way home that night, Hedgehog saw the unicorn a second time. He ran to fetch the other animals.

"I see it, but I still don't believe it!" Hare said.

"Undeniably, it appears to be a unicorn," said Bear. "However, in all likelihood, it is merely moonlight on the moist leaves, or some such distortion."

"Yes, but look—a unicorn is standing right there. We all can see it with our own eyes!" cried Hedgehog.

The other animals shook their heads.

The next evening, when the animals gathered as usual to tell stories, no one could think of a thing to say. They had forgotten every single story! Baffled, they sat there, looking dumbly at each other.

The next day, the forest, usually so bright and vibrant, was dim and dull. The birds stopped singing. Not even the stream babbled cheerfully anymore. And there was a chill in the air.

It must have something to do with the unicorn," said Hare. "Maybe it really *was* there. But since none of us believed it, it has gone, and nothing is as lovely as it was before."

"Yes," said Bear. "Now I, too, believe that the unicorn was in our woods. Or something very like it. It's possible that our doubt has caused this environmental disturbance."

"Then we have to find the unicorn!" said Badger.

The animals searched everywhere, but they found no unicorn.

Perhaps we should try to lure the unicorn out of hiding," said Owl.

"But with what?" asked Hare. "What does a unicorn eat?"

"I don't think it wants food," said Badger. "Maybe it hides because it's shy. Or maybe it thinks we don't believe in it—or in anything magical anymore. After all, we've forgotten all our wonderful stories."

Then we must think of a new one," said Fox. "Perhaps if we all try, we can come up with something. If each of us can just say one part, maybe we'll create a story together."

Everyone agreed to try.

Owl began, "Once there was a unicorn who loved stories very much."

Then Hare said, "But it was driven away by disbelief and took all memory of stories away with it."

"Then the world became cold and lonely and sad," Badger continued.

"It happened on a day when the unicorn went to the stream to drink," said Fox. "Hedgehog saw the wonderful animal and ran to tell his friends."

Already the evening air was not quite so cold. A nightingale began to sing. And from the stream came a cheerful babble, the music of water on stones.

The animals didn't look up. They just kept telling the story as if they didn't notice the changes. But they all rejoiced inside.

When the moon glazed the treetops, the animals headed home. Hare accompanied Hedgehog part of the way. When they came to the stream, they saw the unicorn drinking again.

Hare wanted to cry out, "I don't believe it!" but Hedgehog nudged him and Hare clapped his paws over his mouth.

The unicorn lifted its head in the moonlight. It looked calm and at peace, as if it felt at home.

Hedgehog welled with happiness at the sight. Silently, he nodded good night to Hare and went on his way.

A Note

The unicorn, from the Greek *monoceros*, probably has its origins in the Orient.

Legends about it have been maintained in the oral traditions of the East. In ancient Persia, the unicorn was a symbol of purity, power, and strength. In China, it is a symbol of virtue. In Christianity, the unicorn symbolizes strength, purity, and love.

The spiral horn in the middle of its forehead has often stood for intellectual strength. Frequently seen as an heraldic beast on banners, the unicorn is also used as an emblem for pharmacies, since its horn was reputed to have medicinal properties, such as being an antidote to poison.

It has been said that the unicorn can be tamed if it lays its head in the lap of a maiden. This legend is represented in important works of art of the Virgin Mary with the unicorn.

If you want to see a unicorn now, you can look up at the night sky where the unicorn appears as a constellation of stars. Or you can discover it in this book, for the famous, albeit shy, story-loving mythological animal sat as a model for the paintings. Truly.

First published in Switzerland under the title *Das sagenhafte Einhorn*.

First published in the United States, Great Britain, Canada, Australia, and New Zealand
in 2004 by North-South Books, an imprint of Nord-Süd Verlag AG,
Gossau Zürich, Switzerland.

Distributed in the United States by North-South Books Inc., New York.
Library of Congress Cataloging-in-Publication Data is available.
A CIP catalogue record for this book is available from The British Library.
ISBN 0-7358-1961-0 (TRADE EDITION)
1 3 5 7 9 HC 10 8 6 4 2
ISBN 0-7358-1962-9 (LIBRARY EDITION)
1 3 5 7 9 LE 10 8 6 4 2
Printed in Denmark

For more information about our books, and the authors and artists
who create them, visit our web site: www.northsouth.com